AVA
AN
WIS
TH

AVA TREE
AND THE
WISHES THREE

BY JEANNE BETANCOURT

ILLUSTRATED BY ANGELA DOMINGUEZ

Feiwel and Friends   New York

A Feiwel and Friends Book
An Imprint of Macmillan

Library of Congress Cataloging-in-Publication Data Available

ISBN-13: 978-0-312-37760-1
ISBN-10: 0-312-37760-6

Design by Barbara Grzeslo and Rich Deas

Feiwel and Friends logo designed by Filomena Tuosto

First Edition: April 2009

Printed in March 2009 in the United States of America by
RR Donnelley, Harrisonburg, Virginia

10 9 8 7 6 5 4 3 2 1

www.feiwelandfriends.com

For Nicole, Pilar, and Biulu,
my three wishes come true.
—J. B.

To my family, friends, and people
with quirky personalities.
—A. D.

CONTENTS

AVA TREE
AND THE
WISHES
THREE

PART ONE

HAPPY
BIRTHDAY
TO
ME

My alarm clock is a rabbit. A real rabbit.

First, I feel a warm, wet nose sniffing my face. As soon as I open my eyes, the rabbit hops all over my bed and me.

The rabbit is Tibbar. Tibbar is the pet of me, Ava Tree.

When Tibbar woke me up the morning of my eighth birthday, I felt sad. My parents died in a car accident when I was six years old. Now, it's just me and my brother Jack in our family. And Tibbar, of course.

A tear rolled down my cheek.

Being an orphan is the saddest thing in my whole life so far, and probably forever.

Tibbar hates when I cry. So that morning, he did the craziest rabbit dance ever. First, he hopped over my legs. Next, he jumped from one foot to another and shook his head. His ears flapped around his head. It made me laugh. The harder I laughed, the faster Tibbar hopped. Those ears were floppity-flopping all over the place.

I sat up. "Good morning, Tibbar," I said.

Tibbar stopped hopping and twitched his whiskers at me.

Tibbar loves it when I talk to him. I think he wishes he could talk people-talk. I wish that, too, sometimes.

"It's the first day of summer vacation," I told Tibbar. "And it's my birthday. We're going to have lots of fun today. We're making a birthday

party for me, Ava Tree. It's going to be a Back-ward, Upside-Down, Inside-Out Birthday Party. I invited everyone in my class to it."

Tibbar tugged at the corner of my pajama sleeve with his mouth. That's Tibbar talk for, "Come on. Get out of bed. Feed me."

We went to the kitchen.

Jack was making breakfast. Everyone says Jack and I look alike. We both have short dark hair and big brown eyes. Our noses are short and straight — just like Mom's.

"Happy B-day, A," Jack said.

Jack loves the alphabet. He uses letters instead of whole words whenever he can.

"What are you cooking?" I asked.

"Your favorite breakfast. B-berry pancakes," he answered.

"I can cook them," I said. "I make very excellent blueberry pancakes."

"You're not making breakfast on your B-day,

A," said Jack. "No one should make their own breakfast on their B-day. It's one of those rules about life."

"One of *your* rules about life," I said.

My brother is a computer whiz. He makes Web sites for people. His office is in the front of our house. Plus, he goes to college. Jack goes to his office in the house every workday at 9 o'clock. No matter what. That's another one of his rules about life.

Tibbar hopped over to his eating corner next to the refrigerator. I filled his eating bowl with kibble.

Jack put a plate with three pancakes on the table. They spelled out my name — AVA. That was what my Mom used to make for me on my birthdays.

Jack pointed to his pile of pancakes. "Mine are Os," he said.

"Because they are 'O, so delicious?'" I asked.

"Correct," he answered.

While we ate our yummy pancakes, Tibbar munched on his kibble.

"Aren't you going to be late for work?" I asked Jack.

"A little," he answered. "The boss said it was OK because it's your birthday."

I poured syrup on my last pancake. "And because you're the boss," I said.

"Because," he agreed.

DON'T
FORGET
TO FLUSH

After Jack went to his office, I cleaned up for my party.

First, I swept the kitchen floor.

Next, I cleaned out Tibbar's litter box. He goes to the bathroom in the litter box. Like a cat.

When I was throwing away the old litter, half of it spilled on the clean kitchen floor.

"Tibbar," I said in a scolding voice, "your litter box is a lot of trouble."

Tibbar looked up from eating a lettuce leaf. His ears drooped. His little pink eyes blinked. He thumped his back legs. I had upset him. I hate when I do that.

"Oh, Tibbar," I said in a nicer voice, "I'm sorry I yelled."

He still looked sad. So I stroked his head and tapped my foot. Tibbar likes it when I tap my foot. I think it reminds him of his mom thumping her rabbit feet.

As I tapped my foot, I said, "I just wish that you would use the toilet like a person, Tibbar."

Suddenly, Tibbar's ears perked up and he hoppity-hopped to the bathroom.

I followed him.

He jumped up on the edge of the toilet seat.

I was afraid he would fall in, so I reached out to rescue him.

But Tibbar didn't need to be rescued.

He needed to go to the bathroom.

And he did.

In the toilet.

I was very surprised to see a rabbit use the toilet.

I ran into Jack's office to tell him what Tibbar did.

Jack said, "Maybe Mom did it. Maybe it's a birthday present from her."

"If she did," I said, "it's a super-nice present."

"She's the best mom," said Jack. "And the best magician."

"The best," I agreed.

Mom was a real magician. She did magic shows at parties and fairs.

"And Dad is the best dad," said Jack. "And the best doctor."

Jack and I talk like that. We both believe that Mom and Dad are still taking care of us.

I didn't care that I had to clean up the litter mess anymore. And I was finished with being sad on my birthday.

* * *

At two o'clock, Jack came into the kitchen backward. His shirt, pants, and jacket were on backward.

Here's the best part: Jack wore a mask of his own face on the back of his head.

"Perfect. Amazing. Fantastic!" I shouted.

"I look OK?" Jack said.

"You look super-duper A-OK," I said.

He put a cake box on the table. "Check out your cake, A."

I opened the box and looked inside.

"Happy Birthday Ava," was written in dark purple frosting letters on top of the cake — backward. AVA YAꓷHTЯi8 YꟼꟼAH

I hugged Jack's back. "Thank you for my backward cake. I love it."

Jack put another box on the table. "Here's another present."

I took the lid off the box. There was a pile of photographs inside. The first one was the face of me, Ava Tree. Under my picture were face photos of every kid coming to my Backward Birthday Party.

"How did you get everybody's face?" I asked.

"I copied them from your class picture," he answered. "Then I blew them up on the computer and printed them out."

"You're my favorite brother," I said.

He grinned. "And your only brother. Get

the scissors. We'll make these pictures into masks."

We cut around the faces. Next, we attached rubber bands on the ears. Those masks were perfect for my Backward Birthday Party.

By three o'clock, everything was ready.

A big tray of inside-out, ham-and-cheese sandwiches sat on the table.

Streamers decorated the floor.

Purple and red balloons hung upside down.

We put a big bouquet of flowers in the middle of the table. The flowers were in the water and the stems stuck upward.

The paper plates and cups were upside down on the table.

Jack and I stood in the middle of the room and admired our work.

"Looks A-OK," said Jack.

"Yeah," I agreed. "Triple A-OK. I'm going to get Priscilla. She should be the first one at my party."

IT WOULD BE MOST IMPROPER

Priscilla Purhfect is my very best friend. We are so lucky because her house is behind my house. Our backyards touch.

Jack said, "I bet Mother Purhfect won't let Priscilla wear her clothes backward."

"That's what I think, too," I agreed.

Priscilla's mother is the strictest mother of all my friends' mothers. Everyone calls her Mother Purhfect.

Even Mr. Purhfect calls her that.

Mother Purhfect's middle name should be "Proper." Mother Proper Purhfect. She wants everything to be perfectly proper at all times.

I quickly ran across our backyard, across the Purhfects' backyard, and onto their back porch.

I knocked on the kitchen door.

Priscilla opened it.

She was wearing a pink silk dress with white lace trim. Her red curly hair sparkled with tiny white-and-silver butterfly clips. Her shoes were shiny black. Her white socks were trimmed with pink lace.

She looked very pretty — like the perfect girl. Only one thing was wrong. Nothing was backward.

"My mother won't let me," Priscilla said in a small, sad voice. "She said it isn't proper."

Mother Purhfect walked into the kitchen. "I most certainly will not allow Priscilla to wear that beautiful dress inside out and backward."

Mother Purhfect shook a finger in my direction. "Ava Tree," she scolded, "your invitation was not correct. The information was not in the proper order."

"But it was supposed to be backward," I protested.

"Not proper. Not proper," she insisted. "You should have asked me for help, dear."

She looked me up and down. I had on jeans and a black T-shirt. The T-shirt had gold stars across the front.

Nothing I had on was backward.

"I'm not dressed for the party yet," I said.

Mother Purhfect put her hands on my shoulders. "I know it's difficult for you," she said in a kinder voice. "You don't have your dear mother to help you plan a birthday celebration. But it's not too late to save this party. I am going to attend it myself. We will have a perfectly lovely, proper little girl's party. Don't you worry, Ava Tree. Mother Purhfect will fix everything."

My heart stopped beating. Mother Purhfect would ruin my party. She would fix everything by trying to make it forward, upside-up right, down-side down, and right-side out.

"Jack is fixing everything," I said. "He's the adult."

"Hardly, my dear," said Mother Purhfect. "He's still a child himself."

"But Jack is twenty-two years old," I protested.

"He still acts like a child," Mother Purhfect said as she took off her apron. "I'll just change into something more festive."

She left the kitchen and headed upstairs.

"My mother will ruin your Backward Party," Priscilla whispered.

"I know," I whispered back. "I wish she wouldn't come."

I tapped my foot to help myself think. What could we do to stop Mother Purhfect from coming to my party? Nothing. I still wished that she wouldn't come.

Suddenly, Mother Purhfect was back in the kitchen. There was a strange, dreamy look on her face.

"I won't be attending your party after all, Ava Tree," she said. "I don't want to interfere with your backward, upside-down, inside-out fun. Such a clever idea." She giggled. "And most improper."

My mouth opened in surprise, but no words came out. I was speechless.

Mother Purhfect backed out of the kitchen. "Priscilla, dear," she said, "don't forget to turn your dress inside out and put it on backward."

"Why did she change her mind?" Priscilla whispered. "She never changes her mind."

"I don't know," I said. "But let's get out of here before she changes it again."

Priscilla grabbed a present bag off the kitchen table. I took her other hand and we ran out of her house and through our two backyards.

I was so excited that I felt like I was flying back to my house. I knew why Mother Purhfect changed her mind. It was because I wished it. My second wish on my birthday had come true.

Could I make more? I wondered.

We went to my room to put our clothes on inside out and backward.

I wondered if I should tell Priscilla about my two wishes coming true. Part of me wanted to tell. But another part of me didn't. I listened to the part of me that said, "Sh-sh! Don't tell."

Priscilla said, "I can't believe my mother changed her mind. And she giggled. She *never* giggles."

"Jack says it's important to change your mind sometimes," I told Priscilla. "He says, 'Changing your mind is good for your health. It's one of those rules about life.'"

I took off my jeans and put on my blue skirt — backward. The silver moon and stars from the front of the skirt were on my backside. I put my silver shirt on inside out over it.

I thought Priscilla and I looked great.

"What if my mother comes to the party, after all?" said Priscilla.

"Keep your fingers crossed," I said. "Backward."

We went downstairs to wait for everyone else to come to my Backward Birthday Party.

IF YOU THINK IT'S DUMB, DON'T COME

"If Reed ruins my party, I will never forgive him," I told Priscilla.

"I wish he wasn't coming," she said. "He's so bossy."

"And mean," I added.

Reed was the only kid in my class that I didn't like.

I straightened Priscilla's mask.

"Reed is always pushing little kids around," she said.

"I know," I agreed.

"Why'd you invite him then?" Priscilla asked.

"Your mother said I had to. She said, 'Miss Ava Tree, you cannot exclude one person when everyone else in the class is invited.' Remember?"

"It would be most improper, Ava Tree," said Priscilla with a grin.

"So I asked Jack if I could 'exclude one person,'" I told Priscilla. "He said, 'You can't leave just one kid out. It's rude. That's one of those rules about life.'"

Priscilla and I were both good at imitating Mother Purhfect and Jack.

The doorbell rang.

"Someone's here," Priscilla said. "I hope it's not my mother."

"I hope it's not Reed," I said as I backed up to the door.

I reached behind myself to open it.

It wasn't Mother Purhfect.

And it wasn't Reed.

It was Tilly.

Tilly is a person with excellent ideas. Her excellent idea for backward dressing was to make her ponytail on her forehead. Her backward T-shirt had the design of a shirt and tie. That was another excellent idea.

When Tilly backed in, Priscilla and I said "Good-bye," instead of "Hello."

We said "Good-bye" whenever somebody new came in.

Priscilla helped everyone put on a backward face mask.

They all loved the masks.

Tilly said, "That was an excellent idea."

"It was Jack's idea," I admitted.

Jack took a bow, backward.

At four o'clock, the official starting time of my Backward Birthday Party, fifteen out of seventeen kids were in my living room.

Jack held up Reed Dimster's and Peter Lamb's

face masks. "Where are these guys?" he asked.

"I saw Peter on my way here," answered Todd. "He was going to pick up Reed. I guess they're late."

I didn't mind if Peter came to my party. Peter was OK most of the time. But I didn't want Reed to come.

I remembered that two wishes I made on my birthday came true. Tibbar used the toilet. Mother Purhfect didn't come to my party. Could I wish for anything I wanted on my birthday and have it come true? It couldn't hurt to try.

I said to myself, *I wish that Reed Dimster does not come to my party.*

I remembered something. When I made the other two wishes, I had tapped my foot. So I did it again.

Nobody knew what I wished. Nobody but me, Ava Tree.

"Ava, I have an excellent idea," said Tilly.

"What's your excellent idea?" I asked.

"Start opening your presents," she answered. "That's what you do last at a party. This is the beginning of your party. So, it will be a backward thing to do."

Tilly handed me a present. "Open mine first," she said.

Tibbar hopped over to watch.

Tilly's present was wrapped with the paper inside out. I took it off. There was gold ribbon tied around the present, under the paper. I crumbled the paper into a ball and threw it across the room for Tibbar.

We all watched him hop after it. He loves to play with balled-up paper. My friends love Tibbar. He is very popular.

I untied the ribbon and opened the box from Tilly. There was another box inside it.

I had to open two smaller boxes to find the present.

It was a pair of silver rabbit earrings with little pink stones for eyes. I put them on right away. Backward.

The next present was from Ryan. It was a mystery book. Everyone knows I love mysteries. Ryan does, too.

"I'll read the last page first," I told him.

"Open mine next," said Priscilla.

Priscilla's present was a small photo album of our school trip to the zoo. The pictures in the album were put in backward.

The first pictures were the ones we took of each other when we got home.

The next picture was of the monkeys. They

were the last animals we saw at the zoo. After that, she had put all the other animals we saw. The last animal picture was of the seals. They were the first animals we saw.

"I love it!" I said.

The doorbell rang.

"Reed," Priscilla and Tilly said in unison.

"And Peter," added Janice.

THE BIGGEST WISH OF ALL

Jack opened the door.

Peter walked in backward. He had on a
T-shirt and base-
ball cap. Both
were on back-
ward. He wore
a pair of sun-
glasses on the
back of his
head.

We all yelled, "Good-bye, Peter!"

He said, "Good-bye! Unhappy Birthday, Ava."

Everyone laughed.

Part of me wasn't laughing, though. That part was thinking, *Reed will walk in behind Peter.*

But Reed didn't walk in.

Peter handed me a note.

"It's from Reed," he said. "He isn't coming. This morning he said he was. But he just changed his mind. It was weird."

My third wish *did* come true after all. Reed Dimster wasn't coming to my Backward Birthday Party.

I opened his note. The letters were all backward. I held it up to the living room mirror. "I'm not coming to your dumb party. Reed."

"Look," Priscilla said, "Reed's name spelled backward is 'deer'."

"It is," I giggled. I imagined Reed Dimster as Rudolph the Red-Nosed Reindeer.

But I didn't keep that idea in my head. I had two other ideas to think about.

One was: *Reed's note is clever.* That surprised me.

The other idea was a question: *Can I wish anything I want in the whole world today and have it come true?*

Jack brought in my birthday cake and everyone sang, "You to, Birthday Happy." It was really hard to do. They had to start over three times.

Backward Jack held out the cake to backward me. "Blow out the candles and make a wish," he said.

I remembered how Tibbar used the toilet when I wished it. How Mother Purhfect changed her mind about coming to my party when I wished it. And how Reed Dimster didn't come to my party when I wished it. Now it was time to make my official birthday cake wish.

There was something that I wanted more than anything else in the world. I would make it my birthday cake wish.

I looked over my shoulder and took a deep breath. Then I tapped my right foot as I thought, *I wish my mother and father weren't dead.* I blew out those candles in one breath.

While Jack cut the cake, I looked around the room. My heart was pounding. Was my

wish going to work? Would my Mom and Dad come back to life?

How would it happen? Would they come in a car? Or would they just suddenly appear?

"Hey, A," Jack said. "Don't you like your cake?"

I looked around the table. Everyone but me had finished eating a piece of cake.

I took a bite. "It's yummy," I said.

But I wasn't thinking about the cake. I was thinking about the wish. My other wishes came true right away. The wish about my parents wasn't coming true. I thought, *Maybe it is too big a wish.* After all, wishing someone isn't dead is a lot bigger than wishing someone doesn't come to a birthday party.

"What are we going to do next?" Peter asked.

"If we're doing the party backward," said Tilly, "games and stuff like that should be next."

"Exactly right," I said. I felt sad because my big wish was not coming true. But I tried to sound happy. I wanted everyone to have fun at my party.

I stood up. "Everybody walk backward through the kitchen to the backyard for a backward race."

After the race, we told jokes backward. I told a knock-knock joke. Priscilla knew it because we tell knock-knock jokes all the time. It was really hard to tell backward.

Me: Police let me in.

Priscilla: Police who?

Me: Police.

Priscilla: Who's there?

Me: Knock, knock.

My favorite backward jokes were the elephant jokes.

Peter had a good one.

Answer: Because your nose touches the ceiling.

Question: How do you know there is an elephant under your bed?

The last thing at my Backward Birthday Party was to eat inside-out sandwiches and drink apple juice.

When the party was over, I said "Hello" to everyone.

And they left.

Everyone but Priscilla. She stayed to help Jack and me clean up.

I didn't tell Jack about the other wishes I made on my birthday that came true. Or the biggest wish I made when I blew out my candles. The one wish that didn't come true.

I didn't tell Priscilla about my wishing power, either.

My birthday wishes were a secret.

When I got in bed that night, Tibbar jumped on the bed and flicked his little tongue on my cheek. I kissed the top of his head and said, "Good night, Tibbar."

He hopped off the bed and into Mom's top hat from her magic show. That's where Tibbar likes to sleep.

I looked out the window at the starry night. "Good night, Dad. Good night, Mom. I love you."

PART TWO

ALPHABET
CEREAL

Tibbar thinks hopping all over a sleeping person is fun. Especially if that person is me, Ava Tree.

I opened my eyes and flipped one of his floppy ears.

Tibbar stopped hopping and waited for me to say good morning to him. Like I always do.

"Good morning, silly rabbit," I said.

A thought came into my head. *Yesterday was my birthday. I had wishing power the whole day.*

Will I have wishing power today, too?

A second thought popped into my head. *Today is the day of the Sterling Park Pet Show.*

"You ready to win another ribbon, Tibbar?" I asked.

Two first prize ribbons for Best Trick were on my bulletin board. Tibbar won them both.

The first year, he hopped through a big hoop two times.

The next year, he hopped through the hoop three times.

It was time for a new trick. I looked over at Mom's top hat from the magic show. *Will Tibbar do the disappearing-rabbit-in-the-hat trick for me?* I wondered.

"Tibbar," I said. "Today we are going to be in a pet show. Are you ready to do a new trick?"

Tibbar jumped off the bed and into Mom's top hat.

Sometimes I think that Tibbar can read my mind.

"That's right," I said. "I want you to do the hat trick. Like you did with Mom."

Tibbar hopped out of the hat and back on the bed. He tugged at my pajama sleeve. Time for breakfast. Practicing magic tricks for the pet show would have to wait.

Jack was eating a bowl of alphabet cereal.

That's his favorite kind.

He stuck a cereal letter to his index finger and showed it to me. "What is this letter?" he asked.

"Q," I answered. I knew what was coming next.

"Let's test how fast you can think of ten words that begin with Q," he said. "It'll be a *quiz*." He looked at the kitchen clock. "Go."

"Quiz," I said. "Question. And queen." My stomach growled with hunger. "And quiet. That's all I can think of. I'm hungry."

"Quitter," he said with a grin. "You did four Q words in three seconds. Not bad."

Jack put his empty bowl in the dishwasher. "Time to go to the office," he said. He patted me on the head. "You set for the day?"

"I'm set," I said. "The pet show is today. I'm going with Priscilla. And Tibbar."

"Priscilla doesn't have a pet," said Jack.

"Mother Purhfect says pets are messy," I said. "I can't even bring Tibbar inside their house. Priscilla wants a cat more than anything in her whole life. She says when she grows up, she's going to have three cats, a dog, and maybe a rabbit."

"Children should have pets," said Jack. "Even if it's only a turtle or a fish. It's one of those rules about life."

I poured myself some orange juice. "That's a rule I believe," I said.

"I'll order us a pizza for dinner tonight," said Jack. "OK?"

"Can we have meatballs on it?" I asked.

"That suits me to a T," he said. "Pizza with M."

"Remember that 'M' is for meatball, not mushroom," I said. "I hate mushrooms."

Sometimes it's tiresome to have a brother who is in love with the alphabet.

After breakfast, I practiced tricks with Tibbar.
We warmed up by doing the hoop trick.

He hopped through the hoop twice. He hopped through the hoop three times. He hopped through it four times.

I gave him a rabbit treat. "You are Super Rabbit, Tibbar," I said.

It was time to try the rabbit-in-the-hat magic trick.

I placed the top hat on the table and put Tibbar in. I waved my hand over the hat like

Mom did for that trick.

I looked inside the hat. Tibbar looked up at me. He was still there.

"You are supposed to disappear," I said. "Just for a minute. Like you did for Mom."

Tibbar jumped out of the hat.

We tried the trick a second time.

Tibbar did not disappear.

The third time I put Tibbar in the hat, I made a wish about it. I said to myself, *Tibbar, I wish you would disappear inside that hat. Do the magic trick.* Then I tapped my right foot a few times.

 I looked in the hat. Tibbar wasn't there. He was gone. Vanished. Dis-appeared.

I was happy. I made a wish and it came true. And it wasn't even my birthday anymore.

It was time to finish the trick.

"Where is that rabbit?" I said, just the way Mom did in her magic show.

It was time for Tibbar to hop out of the hat. But Tibbar did not hop out of the hat.

I looked in the hat.

No Tibbar.

I shook the hat upside down.

Nothing.

No rabbit.

Where was my Tibbar? Did I disappear him forever?

"Come out of the hat, Tibbar Tree," I said sternly. My voice was shaking, I was so scared.

Still no Tibbar.

THE
DISAPPEARED
RABBIT

I looked inside the empty hat again. *Maybe I have to wish him back,* I thought.

"I wish you would come back, Tibbar," I said. I tapped my foot again.

Tibbar jumped out of the hat.

Just like that.

He hopped all over the kitchen table. I was so happy that I hopped around with him.

When we finished our rabbit hop, I sat down at the table to think things over. A bunch of thoughts came into my brain, one after another.

First thought: *I will not try the rabbit-in-the-hat magic trick at the Sterling Park Pet Show. I'm not going to mix up magic tricks with wishes. Jumping through hoops is a good-enough normal animal trick. Tibbar can do it without any wishing help from me.*

Second thought: *I can make wishes and they will come true. Even on my un-birthday.*

Third thought: *I have to say exactly what I want in a wish. Otherwise, something awful could happen. Like my rabbit disappearing forever.*

My fourth thought was a question: *Do my wishes last?*

I remembered my first wish on my birthday. I wished that Tibbar would use the toilet and he did. *Will Tibbar use the toilet all the time now?* I wondered.

Just then, Tibbar hopped over to his litter box and used it. That told me that my first wish did not last.

The cuckoo clock in the kitchen cuckooed ten times.

Ten o'clock! It was time to go to Priscilla's.

I put Tibbar's leash on him and we went out the back door. We walked through our backyard, the Purhfects' backyard, and onto their back porch.

I could hear Mother Purhfect scolding Pris-

cilla through the screen door. "I can't believe you wore that beautiful dress inside out and backward."

"But Mother, you said — " Priscilla began.

"Do not interrupt, Priscilla Purhfect," Mother Purhfect said. "And eating cake first. That kind of behavior is totally unacceptable."

Mother Purhfect didn't think backward birthday parties were a good idea anymore. My second birthday wish hadn't lasted, either.

I tied Tibbar's leash to the railing. I couldn't let Priscilla take the scolding alone.

I went into the house.

"Well, there you are, Ava Tree," Mother Purhfect said. "Your birthday party was most improper."

"I promise I won't have a Backward Birthday Party next year," I said.

"You certainly will not," Mother Purhfect said. "Next year, I will help right from the beginning. We will have a nice tea party just for the young ladies. It will be very proper. And I will buy the invitations."

Priscilla was standing behind her mother. She rolled her eyes. I couldn't laugh because Mother Purhfect was looking right at me.

"Won't that be lovely, Ava Tree?" Mother Purhfect said.

"Lovely," I agreed.

I hope that next year I still have wishing power. I will need it if I want to have a good birthday party.

SCRAPPY AND BIG BOY

I love the Sterling Park Pet Show. It's a very popular event in our town.

Tibbar is happy whenever we go to Sterling Park. He likes to eat the clover in the grass.

We were only in the park a few minutes when Priscilla grabbed my arm. "Look at that cute adorable kitten," she said.

She was pointing at a black kitten in a small cage. The kitten had white fur around its left eye. Priscilla was right. He was cute adorable.

A sign over the cage read, KITTEN FOR FREE.

A dark-haired girl sat next to the cage.

"We found this kitten in the woods," she said. "My dad won't let me keep her. We already have three cats. But if she stays outside in the winter, she will be so cold and hungry."

"That would be awful," said Priscilla. "She's such a little thing." She held out her hands. "Can I hold her?"

The girl took the kitten out of the cage and handed her to Priscilla. The kitten meowed when she saw Tibbar. Tibbar wanted to play with her, but the kitten was scared and hid under Priscilla's elbow. Maybe that kitten never saw a rabbit before. Or maybe the rabbits in the woods were mean to her.

"Tibbar and I will walk around and see who else is here," I told Priscilla. "You can catch up."

I walked along the path toward the pet show. I was looking for kids and pets that I knew.

Suddenly, two hands reached from behind and covered my eyes.

"Who is it?" I asked. "Is it you, Tilly?"

Tilly was entering her hamsters, Max and Ruby, in the pet show.

"Guess again," said the joker in a funny, made-up voice.

It could be a girl or a boy, I thought.

"Ryan?" I asked.

I knew Ryan was coming with his cat, Fargo.

"I suppose *Ryan* was at your stupid birthday party," said the joker in his real voice.

I yanked the hands off my eyes and whipped around. Reed. Tall, skinny, mean Reed Dimster.

Peter was with him. So was Reed's black Lab, Big Boy. Big Boy is sweet and well-behaved — unlike his owner.

Tibbar and Big Boy sniffed noses. Tibbar is not afraid of any other animals — even big ones. He is a very unusual rabbit.

"It was a fan-tas-tic party," I told Reed. "Everyone had a great time. Tell him, Peter."

"It was dumb," Peter said. He was looking at the ground when he said that. He knew it was a lie. And he knew that I knew it was a lie.

I glared at him. "Liar," I said.

"Not," he mumbled.

I hate how Peter acts when he is with Reed. He thinks Reed is this big deal and tries to act like him.

Priscilla caught up with us. "If that kitten was my kitten I would name her Precious. I wish I could take her home."

"'If that kitten was my kitten I would name her Precious. I wish I —'" said Reed, mimicking Priscilla.

"Stop it, Reed," said Priscilla.

"'Stop it, Reed,'" said Reed.

"Reed is a jerk," I said.

"'Reed is —'" Reed began. He stopped

before saying that he was a jerk. *"You're* the jerks," he said. "Let's go, Pete."

Big Boy gave Tibbar one last sniff and followed the boys.

"Precious is a perfect name for that kitten," I told Priscilla.

A little girl and her dog were coming toward us. The dog was light brown with brown spots. The girl had light brown hair, too.

The dog looked odd because one ear was smaller than the other. Two of his teeth came over his lip. He was funny looking, but in a cute way.

Reed noticed the girl and her dog. He laughed his mean laugh. "That's an ugly excuse for a dog," he told the little girl.

"That dog couldn't win *anything*," added Peter.

"Yes, it could," said Reed. "It could win first prize for Ugliest Pet."

Reed and Peter kept walking. The little girl leaned over and hugged her dog. "I love you, Scrappy," she said. Tears filled her eyes. She gave a little tug on Scrappy's leash. "Come on. We're going home."

I went over to them. I was having an excellent idea about what to do with my next wish.

"Those boys are bullies," I told the little girl. "Don't let them keep you and Scrappy out of the pet show." I turned to Priscilla. "Isn't that right?"

Priscilla nodded.

"That kitten should be in the show, too," I said. "Everyone should be in the pet show."

"You're right," agreed Priscilla. "Maybe I can borrow the kitten for the show. That way, more people will see her. Someone could adopt her. Someone whose mother will let them."

Priscilla went to see if she could borrow the kitten for the pet show.

I asked Scrappy's owner her name. It was Liz. Tibbar cheered Liz up by hopping around.

CUTEST
KITTEN

The six of us entered the Sterling Park Pet Show. Scrappy and Liz. The kitten and Priscilla. Tibbar and me. The kitten wasn't afraid of Tibbar anymore.

"That's a very adaptable kitten," I told Priscilla.

This year, there were sixteen dogs, thirteen cats, ten hamsters, six guinea pigs, one kitten, and one rabbit in the pet show.

Animal tricks was the first category. A brown

dog, Coffee, tried to catch a Frisbee while it was in the air. He finally caught it on the third try. A yellow cat, Puff, slid down a little kid slide. That was a super-cute trick. Then Tibbar jumped through the hoop four times. The last time he did it *backward*. I didn't even ask him to do it backward. He just did.

Tibbar won first prize. The cat won second prize. And Coffee got the third-prize ribbon.

I was proud of Tibbar when we accepted the ribbon.

"You shouldn't have won, Ava," Reed said.

"Any rabbit can hop through a hoop. That's what rabbits do — hop."

I didn't even look at Reed when he said that. I didn't say anything to him, either. I didn't need to. I knew that Reed Dimster was in for a big surprise.

The next category was Best Looking Cat. Priscilla carried Precious over to the judges.

Precious didn't win Best Looking Cat because she wasn't full-grown.

"But she is the cutest kitten," said the judge. "This kittten wins a blue ribbon in the Cutest Kitten category." He handed Priscilla a first-prize ribbon and a cat toy.

"You mean she wins in the Only Kitten category," Reed shouted out.

A few people laughed.

Priscilla and the kitten didn't care. They were still happy with their ribbon and toy.

"If I owned Precious, I would enter her next year, too," Priscilla told me. "Then she would win in the Best Looking Cat category." She shook her head sadly. "But next year she could be alone in the woods." A tear dripped down her cheek. "Or . . ."

The kitten licked the tear with her little tongue.

"You have to adopt Precious," I told Priscilla. "You two belong together."

"Next category," the judge announced. "Best Looking Dog."

"That's us," Reed told Big Boy.

Big Boy and Reed were the first to walk around the ring.

Next came a black poodle, August, and her owner, Mona. August looked pretty good. But so far, I had to admit, Big

Boy was the best-looking dog.

He was better looking than the next two dogs, too.

"The final dog in this category is Scrappy," the judge announced.

Reed and Peter laughed.

Liz looked up at me. "I can't go out there," she said.

"You can," I said. "You have to for Scrappy. He might win a ribbon and a toy." I put my hand on her shoulder. "He will win. I promise."

The judge told Liz to walk Scrappy around the ring. Scrappy stopped a couple of times to rest. A lot of people laughed when that happened. But it wasn't a mean laugh. It was a friendly laugh.

"Scrappy was the last entry in the Best Looking Dog category," the judge announced.

I tapped my foot a few times and thought, *I wish that Scrappy wins Best Looking Dog.*

"And the best-looking dog is Bi — " The judge hesitated. A dreamy expression came over his face. "Why, the best-looking dog is that dog — " He pointed to Scrappy. "Yes, it's Scrappy. He is a uniquely good-looking dog."

Everyone laughed and clapped. Everyone except Reed and Peter.

Reed shouted out, "Hey, that's not fair. That dog is ugly."

"I will be the judge of that, young man," the judge said sternly. "Scrappy is the best-looking dog. First prize goes to Scrappy and his fine young owner, Liz."

A big grin spread across Liz's face.

I gave her a little push. "Go get your ribbon."

Liz and Scrappy ran up to collect the ribbon and dog toy. Liz put the ribbon on Scrappy's collar.

Everyone clapped again.

Big Boy and the other dogs won ribbons, too. But Scrappy was number one.

Liz came back to our little group. Reed came over, too. "Your dog is the ugliest dog I've ever seen," he told Liz.

"He is not ugly," said Liz. She pointed to the blue ribbon on Scrappy's collar. "He's the best looking. He won first prize."

I gave Big Boy a handful of rabbit treats. He ate them in one happy bite. He didn't care about winning first prize.

The pet show was over. It was time to go home.

I looked around for Priscilla. She was giving the kitten back to the little girl.

I thought about my wishing power. I would make another wish on Mother Purhfect. I would wish she would let Priscilla keep Precious.

Tibbar and I raced over to Priscilla and the girl. I hoped no one else wanted the kitten.

If they do, I thought, *I can make a wish to change their minds.*

I loved making wishes!

NOT
IN THIS
HOUSE

"She'll take it," I told the girl. "Priscilla will take Precious."

"My mother will never let me have a kitten," Priscilla said. "You know that, Ava Tree."

"Don't worry," I said. "She'll change her mind when she meets Precious. She will fall in love with her. Just like you did. I promise."

"You think so?" Priscilla asked. The tears made her eyes shine.

"I know so," I told her.

Priscilla carried the kitten home in her arms.

Precious was very happy to be there. She purred the whole way.

Before we went to Priscilla's house, I brought Tibbar home. He hopped over to the top hat. He was ready for a nap after the pet show. I pinned his new ribbon on the bulletin board.

"See you later, Tibbar," I said.

Priscilla raised Precious's little black paw in the air. "Wave good-bye to your new friend," she said. She moved the kitten's paw up and down.

Tibbar's right ear twitched a tired good-bye.

"Friends forever," said Priscilla.

"Just like us," I said. I grabbed her hand. "Come on, let's go see if your mother is home."

We could see Mother Purhfect in the kitchen through the screen door.

I said to myself, *Mother Purhfect, please let Priscilla keep the kitten.* I tapped my right foot three times.

We walked into the house.

Mother Purhfect saw the kitten right away. She frowned and pointed to the door. "No animals in the house, girls. Certainly you know that by now."

What happened to my wishing power? I wondered. *What did I do wrong? Do I have to look at Mother Purhfect when I make the wish?*

I looked right at Mother Purhfect and thought, *I wish with all my heart that you let*

Priscilla keep the kitten. I tapped my foot.

"But Mother, this kitten needs a home," said Priscilla.

"Not this home," said Mother Purhfect. "No animals means no pets. And no pets means no kittens."

"She will freeze to death in the woods," protested Priscilla. "I have to take care of her."

"It is seventy-five degrees out today, Priscilla Purhfect," Mother Purhfect said. "Nothing is going to freeze."

Mother Purhfect glared at me. "Was this your idea, Miss Tree?"

"Yes, Ma'am," I said. "Precious is a wonderful kitten. She won't bother — "

"There will be no pets in the Purhfect household," Mother said, interrupting me. "No kitten."

Priscilla looked at me. Her eyes filled up with tears again.

"I'll take Precious to my house," I said. "Jack will let me keep her. You can play with her there."

Priscilla handed Precious to me. "But I wanted to take care of her myself," she said.

I held the soft, black kitten in my arm. Precious was still looking at Priscilla. She meowed. That little meow said, "How come I'm not with *you*?"

"It's okay," I told Precious as I walked back to my house. "I will take good care of you."

I was happy to have another pet. But

Precious wasn't my pet. She belonged to Priscilla.

I knew it.

Priscilla knew it.

Even Precious knew it.

How could we make Mother Purhfect know it, too?

I walked up the back porch stairs to my house. *What happened to my wishing power? I wondered. Is it gone?*

PART THREE

A-AMAZING

The next morning, a wet lick woke me up. "Good morning, Tibbar," I said as I opened my eyes.

"Meow."

It wasn't Tibbar.

A little ball of black fur snuggled against my shoulder. Precious.

I petted her tiny head with two fingers. "You sweet kitten," I said. "Priscilla would love to wake up with you every day."

Tibbar crawled out of Mom's top hat and jumped onto the bed. He brushed his lips against my other cheek.

"You're sweet, too, Tibbar," I told him.

I knew that Tibbar would always be my number one pet. I had to make sure that he knew that, too.

I looked over at the new blue ribbon Tibbar won in the Sterling Park Pet Show. "And you are very clever, too, Tibbar," I said.

Tibbar and Precious chased one another over my bedcovers. Tibbar was acting more like a kitten than a rabbit.

I watched them and thought about my wishing power.

On my birthday, I wished that Tibbar would use the toilet. That wish came true. Next, I wished that Mother Purhfect would not come to my party, and she didn't. Then I wished that Reed Dimster would not come to my party.

He didn't come, either. I made those three wishes on my birthday and they all came true.

Yesterday, I used up two wishes on the rabbit-in-the-hat magic trick. I was sorry I tried that trick. It was very scary when Tibbar disappeared. Next, I made a wish that Scrappy would win Best Looking Dog. Three wishes that came true the day after my birthday.

But the next wish I made yesterday did *not* come true. Mother Purhfect would not let Priscilla keep Precious. That was the fourth wish I made yesterday.

I sat up in bed. Maybe I could only make three wishes a day. My heart pounded with excitement. I might still have wishing power! Wishing power for three wishes a day. If I still had wishing power maybe —

I jumped out of bed, tapped my foot, and said to myself, *I wish that Mother Purhfect lets Priscilla keep Precious.*

I couldn't wait to see if that wish would come true.

Tibbar tugged on my pajama sleeve. Time for breakfast.

Precious and Tibbar followed me to the kitchen.

Jack was finishing his alphabet cereal.

"How's that kitten doing?" he asked.

Precious ran over to Jack's feet. She thought his shoelaces were very interesting.

I put out rabbit food for Tibbar and a small bowl of milk for Precious.

Precious looked from Jack's interesting shoelaces to the yummy milk. Back and forth three times.

Jack laughed. "Big decisions have to be made when you are a kitten."

Precious gave up the shoelaces and went over to the milk.

"She is so cute," I said.

"It's too bad that Priscilla can't keep her," said Jack.

Our kitchen screen door flung open.

"I can keep her!" Priscilla shouted as she ran in. "I can have Precious. My mother said."

Priscilla picked up Precious. "You are my very own kitten," she said as she hugged her. "The perfect pet. My Precious."

"Wow!" I said. "That is so great."

Jack patted Priscilla on the shoulder. "That's wonderful, P," he said. "I never thought I'd see the day Mother Purhfect would let you have a pet."

"Me, either," said Priscilla. "At breakfast, I was begging her to let me have Precious. She said, 'No cats. They are too messy. There will never be a kitten or kitty litter in my home.'"

Priscilla stroked the kitten's shiny black coat. "All of a sudden, Mother stopped talking and stared at the floor. Then she said, 'That kitten is very cute. A child should have a pet. So, you can have the kitten.' She even gave me money to buy food and everything I need for Precious."

"A-amazing," said Jack.

It is A-amazing, I thought. *A-amazing that Priscilla can keep Precious. And A-amazing that I still have wishing power.*

Now I was sure that I only had wishing power for three wishes a day. If I made a fourth wish, it wouldn't come true.

A new, very big, humungous thought came into my head: *On my birthday, I made four wishes, too.*

The fourth wish was that my mother and father would be alive again.

I thought, *That's why that wish didn't come true. It was the fourth wish on a three-wish day!*

Maybe wishing my parents were still alive isn't too big a wish after all. I can try that wish again.

Jack was busy emptying the dishwasher.

93

Priscilla was busy playing with Precious.

I tapped my foot, closed my eyes, and made my second wish of the day. *I wish with all my heart and all the wishes of my lifetime that my mother and father are alive again.*

I opened my eyes and looked around the kitchen. *Would they come in through the kitchen door?* I wondered.

They didn't.

Maybe they're upstairs, I thought. *Maybe it's hard to come back to life and they're resting.*

"I'm going upstairs to get dressed," I told Priscilla.

I ran up the stairs and into my parents' old bedroom. The bed was empty.

It was only my second wish of the day and it didn't come true. Suddenly, I knew that that wish would never come true. I could not make people undead — even if I used up all the wishes of my lifetime.

I threw myself on the bed and cried. I felt a small, warm body next to my face.

It was Tibbar. I didn't know he'd followed me upstairs.

Next, I felt a hand on my back. It was Jack.

"What's wrong, A?" he asked.

I sat up. "Sometimes, I miss Mom and Dad so much," I sobbed.

Jack blinked to keep from crying, too. "Yeah," he said. "I know."

He put his arm around me and I leaned my head into his shoulder. Tibbar hopped on my lap. The three of us sat like that for a while.

"You okay now?" Jack asked.

I nodded and dried my tears with my pajama sleeve.

"What are you and Priscilla going to do this morning?" Jack asked.

"We're going to the pet store," I said, "to get stuff for Precious. I better get dressed."

When I went back downstairs, Priscilla was making a list.

THINGS TO BUY FOR PRECIOUS

DRY CAT FOOD
WET CAT FOOD
KITTY LITTER
LITTER BOX
MORE CAT TOYS
CAT CARRIER

Tibbar watched Precious bat around the cat toy she won. Whenever it came close to Tibbar, he batted it away. Precious did all the running around.

That's what they were doing when Priscilla and I left for the pet store.

"Precious and Tibbar will have a lot of play-dates," Priscilla said. Suddenly, she stopped in the middle of the sidewalk. "What if my mother changes her mind?"

What if? I thought. I remembered that my wishes only lasted a day. For Priscilla to keep Precious, I would have to wish it every day.

Every morning, I will wish that Priscilla can keep Precious, I promised myself.

I put an arm around Priscilla's shoulder. "Don't worry about it," I said. "She won't change her mind."

Priscilla would have Precious for as long as I had wishing power.

BELLY FLOPS

We brought Precious and the things from the pet store to Priscilla's house. Mother Purhfect came into the kitchen and saw Precious on Priscilla's lap.

"What a perfectly adorable kitten," Mother Purhfect exclaimed. She picked up the purring kitten and kissed her little furry head. "Absolutely adorable."

Priscilla and I grinned at one another. Mother Purhfect had not changed her mind about Precious.

Mother took two of her prettiest bowls from the cupboard. "Use these for Precious Purhfect's food," she said. "And put the litter box in the downstairs bathroom. That way she won't have to go upstairs to do her business."

Mother Purhfect didn't even mind kitty litter anymore. My wish was working great.

The three of us ate grilled-cheese sandwiches and watched Precious play.

After lunch, Priscilla and I brought Precious to my house for another playdate with Tibbar. Precious ran in happy circles around Tibbar.

Tibbar pretended to be trying to catch her. But mostly, he watched.

In the afternoon, Priscilla and I rode our bikes to the Sterling Park Swimming Pool. It is our favorite summer place.

After we parked our bikes, we went to the locker room to change.

"Are you going to try to dive today?"

Priscilla asked as we headed to the pool.

"Sure," I said.

"You're such a good swimmer," said Priscilla. "It's funny you can't dive."

"Funny weird," I said.

"Ava! Priscilla! Over here!" someone shouted.

I squinted in the sun to see who it was. Tilly. She was sitting at the edge of the pool with her feet dangling in the water.

We ran over and sat on either side of her.

Priscilla told Tilly all about Precious and

how her mother changed her mind. We were getting super hot in the sun.

Priscilla kicked the water. "Let's go in."

"We can practice our dives," said Tilly.

"Okay," agreed Priscilla.

"You, too, Ava," said Tilly. "You have to dive, too."

"I'll try," I said.

Priscilla dove in first. Then Tilly.

It was my turn. They bobbed in the water in front of me.

"Keep your head between your arms," said Tilly.

"And bend your knees to push off," added Priscilla.

I reached my arms over my head and leaned forward.

Ready.

Push off.

Whack!

A belly flop.

And a nose full of water.

"Uh-oh, that hurt," said Priscilla.

We climbed out of the pool. I patted my stinging belly. I didn't feel much like trying again.

"I wish you could dive like us," said Priscilla.

"Me, too," I said. "I wish that, too."

Wish, wish, wish. *That's it,* I thought. *Maybe I can use one of my three wishes for diving.*

I wish that I could dive, I said to myself. I tapped my foot on the ground.

Priscilla dove in.

Tilly dove in.

"Okay, Ava," Tilly shouted. "And remember what we said."

I raised my arms over my head.

Knees bent.

Ready.

Push off.

Hands, arms, head, and body glide smoothly into the water.

I did two breaststrokes under water before I came up for air.

Priscilla and Tilly were swimming toward me.

"That was perfect," said Priscilla.

"Perfect," echoed Tilly. "How did it feel?"

"Great!" I said.

RETSMID
DEER

We dove from the side of the pool again. My wish was still working. I did another perfect dive.

Next, Tilly and Priscilla wanted to dive from the diving board.

"Me, too," I said.

Tilly climbed out of the pool and looked down at me. "You sure?" she said. "Maybe you should dive more from the side first."

I pulled myself out of the water and stood

beside her. "I'm sure I can do it," I said.

We headed for the diving board and stood in line behind two older kids.

Priscilla did an okay dive off the board.

It was Tilly's turn. She walked to the end of the board and balanced on her tiptoes.

"Tilly's a lousy diver," a voice behind me shouted.

I knew that voice. It was Reed Dimster. He was in line right behind me.

Tilly looked around just as she started her dive. It threw off her balance. She did a belly flop.

"Oh, that has to hurt," Reed laughed. He poked me in the back. "Your turn to do a belly flop, Tree."

I turned and pointed my finger at him. "Watch me, Rudolph."

I walked to the end of the board and raised my arms. The diving board started shaking. I almost fell off.

Reed was jumping up and down on the other end of the board.

"Stop it, Reed," Tilly shouted from the water.

A lifeguard's whistle pierced through the pool noise. "No jumping on the board," she scolded through a bullhorn.

The board was still shaking when I rose to my toes and shot into the air. I reached my feet toward the sky and bent my head toward the water. My body sliced into it.

The first person I saw when I came up was Reed. He was looking down at me from the end of the diving board. His mouth was opened in surprise.

Priscilla and Tilly swam toward me.

"Wow, Ava," said Priscilla. "That was beautiful."

"You got so high," said Tilly. "It was like the best dive I've ever seen."

Reed jumped off the diving board, hugged

his knees, and cannonballed toward us.

The splash waved over me.

The lifeguard's whistle sang through the air again.

"Break one more pool rule, Dimster," the lifeguard shouted through the bullhorn, "and you are out of here for the season."

"It would serve you right, Rudolph," said Priscilla.

"What's with calling me Rudolph?" he asked. "What's that supposed to mean?"

"You are Rudolph the Red-Nosed Rein*deer*," I said.

Reed wanted to splash us again. But he didn't dare. Not with the lifeguard watching.

"Spell your name backward, Reed," Tilly said.

"R-E-T-S-M-I-D," said Reed. "So what?"

"Try your first name," I said as I pulled myself out of the water.

He shook the water out of his spiky hair. "D-E-E-R," he said. "Deer. Still dumb."

"Not dumb, Rudolph the Red-Nosed Rein-DEER," Tilly teased.

I climbed up the diving board ladder and did another perfect dive from the board.

It felt wonderful to fly through the air and slip into the water. But I felt a little weird about it, too.

As I rose up through the water, I thought, *I really don't know how to dive. My wish is letting me be a good diver. And only for today.*

"Let's get some ice cream," I shouted to Priscilla and Tilly.

We got out of the water, dried off, and headed over to the ice cream truck.

"Ava, did you take secret lessons in diving?" Tilly asked.

"I bet Jack taught her," said Priscilla.

"No," I said. "I just sort of figured it out."

"And you did what we said," added Tilly.

"Right," I agreed. "I did what you said."

"Your mother was a great diver," said Priscilla. "Maybe you inherited it."

"Maybe," I said.

I wondered, *What if my friends knew I really couldn't dive? What if they knew I had wishing power?* I wasn't going to let them find out either of those things about me — Ava Tree.

A BIG RED NOSE

I bought a vanilla ice cream cone with rainbow sprinkles.

Peter was at the ice cream truck, too. A super-cute little girl was holding his hand. She had ponytails sticking out on both sides of her head.

"I want chocolate," the little girl said. "Chocolate, chocolate, chocolate."

"Is that your sister?" Tilly asked Peter.

He nodded.

"My name is Jessie," the little girl said. "But sometimes, I'm Winnie the Pooh. I'm three and three-quarters." She held up four fingers. "That's almost four."

"I have to babysit her all summer," said Peter. "It's my job. I get paid."

"I'm not a baby," Jessie protested. "I'm a big girl. You're big-girl-sitting."

I squatted down in front of Jessie. I always wished I could have a little sister.

"Hi, Jessie," I said. "My name is Ava."

"You had a birthday party," said Jessie. "It was backward and upside down."

"And inside out," added Tilly.

"Peter practiced walking backward," Jessie said. "He bumped into things. I had to help him."

"I was just fooling around," Peter said. He handed Jessie her ice cream cone.

Tilly pointed her ice cream at a bench under a big tree. "Let's go over there," she said to Priscilla and me. "My ice cream's melting."

We headed toward the bench.

Jessie followed us.

Peter followed Jessie.

We sat in the shade and licked our cool ice cream cones. We were all super happy.

"I like summer vacation best at the beginning," said Peter. "Before it starts getting used up."

"Me, too," agreed Tilly.

I saw Reed heading in our direction. A little kid with an ice cream cone was in his way. Instead of going around the kid, Reed bumped into him — on purpose. The kid's ice cream cone fell to the ground.

Reed didn't stop to help the kid. He just laughed and kept going.

I was so mad at Reed that I made a wish about him.

I wish that Reed Dimster's nose turns red like Rudolph the Red-Nosed Reindeer. I tapped my foot hard three times.

I watched Reed's face as he came closer to us.

No red nose.

My wish hadn't worked.

When Reed reached us, his nose was still normal.

"Hey, Tree," he said, "what happened to your nose?"

Everyone turned to look at me.

Priscilla's eyes opened wide.

Tilly's mouth dropped open.

"How come your nose is red?" asked Jessie.

"It's really red," added Peter. "And big."

I felt my nose. It *was* bigger.

I crossed my eyes to look at it. Red. My nose was big and red. Not Reed's.

"What happened, Ava?" asked Priscilla.

"Did something bite you?" asked Tilly.

"Maybe," I said. "I guess."

I knew the truth. My nose wasn't big and red because of an insect bite. It was big and red because my wish about Reed happened to me instead of him.

But why?

It was time to make another wish.

I wish my nose would not be red anymore, I said to myself as I tapped my foot.

"Wow, that's the reddest nose I've ever seen," said Peter.

Still red.

Why can't I turn it back? I wondered. *Will it be like this for the rest of my life?* Then I remembered. I already made three wishes today. The first was so Priscilla could keep Precious. Next, I wished that my parents would come back. But that wish didn't work, so I still should have two left. I used one for diving and one for making Reed's nose red. That was the wish that turned around and made my nose red instead.

Three wishes all used up. I remembered that my wishes only lasted a day. *I have to wait until tomorrow*, I thought, *for my nose to go back to normal.*

Reed started humming "Rudolph the Red-Nosed Reindeer."

"Maybe your brother should bring you to a doctor?" said Tilly.

"Or we could go to my house and show my mother," said Priscilla. "She'll know what to do."

"No," I said. "I'm sure it will go away by tomorrow. I'm going home now."

"I'll come with you," said Priscilla.

"You don't have to," I said. "Stay and swim some more."

Priscilla put her arm around my shoulder. "I'm coming with you," she said. "We can play with Precious and Tibbar. Let's go."

Priscilla is absolutely my best friend.

We said good-bye to everyone.

Reed sang, "Rudolph the Red-Nosed Ava Tree," as we walked away.

"I wish Reed was the one with the red nose," said Priscilla.

"Yeah," I agreed. "I wish that, too."

I looked in the mirror as soon as I got home. Very red. Very, very, very red. And big.

Priscilla and I sat in my living room to play with Tibbar and Precious. Precious climbed all over Priscilla.

Tibbar rested quietly on my lap. I guess he was tired out from playing with the frisky kitten. I scratched behind his ears. Tibbar especially likes it when I do that.

"So many weird things have been happening lately," Priscilla said. "First of all, my mother changed her mind about your party. She never changes her mind."

"Maybe she's changed her mind about never changing her mind," I said.

"I don't think so," said Priscilla. "Then when we didn't want Reed to come to your party, he didn't." She sat up. "And Scrappy won the Best Looking Dog contest. Just before he won, I thought, I wish Scrappy would win. And he did. It was like everything we wished for came true. It's kind of spooky."

Priscilla was thinking about wishing power, too. I didn't want her to figure out that I had it.

"It's all just a lucky coincidence," I said.

I put Tibbar on the floor and stood up. "Hey," I said, "let's have some leftover birthday cake."

Jack came into the kitchen while we were eating cake. "Whoa, A," he said when he saw me. He came up close to my nose. "That's some bite."

Jack made me hold ice on my nose for ten minutes. Then he put on special bug bite medicine.

"This is what Dad always put on our bites," he said as he rubbed it in.

"I think it will be better in the morning," I told Jack.

MIDNIGHT SNACK

That night when I got in bed, I thought about everything that had happened to me in the last three days.

I definitely had wishing power. Me, Ava Tree. But why? And where did the power come from? Having wishing power was confusing. I was feeling bad.

Tibbar jumped on the bed and lay next to me. He does that when I'm upset. Tibbar is a very sensitive rabbit.

I touched my nose. It was still swollen. "I'm

not going to wish any more mean things," I told Tibbar.

Tibbar licked my face and snuggled closer.

I thought some more about my wishing power. Was I going to have it every day of my life?

It was hot in my room. I got up and opened the window.

A sweet, summer wind blew in. I sat in my rocker and watched the moon-and-stars mobile over my bed sway in the breeze.

Tibbar hopped onto my lap. I rocked him and hummed, "Rock-a-bye Baby."

I hadn't thought about that song in years. It was the lullaby my mother sang to me when I was little. Only, Mom used her own words. The words popped into my head, so I sang them to Tibbar.

Rock-a-bye baby, in my arms here.
Go to sleep, Ava, mother is near.

Good days and sad days. Happy or blue.
Mother will see that your wishes come true.

Close your eyes, Ava, this day is done.
Someday you will have great wishing fun.
Wish for what's good. Wish for what's right.
Now, my dear child, I wish you good night.

I sang the song through a second time. Did my mother know that someday I would have wishing power? The lullaby made me think that the answer to that question was "Yes."

I couldn't go to sleep after that. I sat looking out the window and thinking about my mother and father and how much I missed them.

I remembered some of the wonderful times I had with them. Mom and Dad skated with Jack and me in the winter and took us camping in the summer. They said they'd rather do things with us than anybody else.

As I thought about the good times we had as a family, it almost felt like my parents were there in the room with me.

I fell asleep in the chair humming the lullaby to myself.

When I woke up, it was still night. Tibbar woke up, too. I was hungry. "There's one slice of meatball pizza left from dinner," I told Tibbar. "And a carrot for you."

I put on my bathrobe and Tibbar and I went down to the kitchen.

While I was finishing up my slice, I noticed that the light was still on in Jack's office. It wasn't like Jack to leave a light on. One of his rules about life is, Turn off the lights when you leave a room.

I looked at the kitchen clock. Ten minutes past midnight. Was Jack still working?

I went down the hall to find out.

He was sitting at his computer, but the screen was blank.

He looked up when I came in. "How come you're up, A?" he asked.

"Hungry," I answered.

"There's that leftover pizza," he said as he looked back to the computer.

"Not anymore," I said. "I just ate it."

Jack hit a few keys on the keyboard. The screen was still blank.

"How come you're still up?" I asked. "I thought one of your rules is, Work only during working hours."

"Right," he agreed. "But another rule is, There are exceptions to all of the rules. Like when your computer breaks down and you have an important client first thing in the morning."

Jack hit a few more keys on his keyboard. The screen was still blank.

It's after midnight, I thought. *A new day. A new day with three wishes in it.* Maybe I could solve Jack's problem.

I tapped my foot and said to myself, *I wish that Jack's computer works again.*

A second later, Jack's computer screen lit up.

"It's back," Jack exclaimed. "A-awesome, A. You brought me good luck. Just like Mom. She was my lucky charm."

Jack touched his nose. "Your nose isn't red and swollen anymore."

I felt my nose and crossed my eyes. Jack was right. My nose was back to normal.

"You fixed it," I said. "Just like Dad. He was my favorite doctor."

Jack got up from his chair and pulled me into a hug.

"If we *are* like Mom and Dad," he said, "it's like they are still with us — in a way. And if that's true, we'll be okay."

"Yeah," I agreed.

I went back to my room and got under the covers. I looked out the open window at the

half moon and twinkling stars. "Good night, Dad. Good night, Mom. Thanks for giving me such a great brother."

Tibbar jumped up next to me to say good night, too. I put my cheek against his soft fur. "Jack is right," I told him. "We will be okay."

Thank you for reading
this FEIWEL AND FRIENDS book.

The Friends who made

AVA TREE AND THE WISHES THREE

possible are:

Jean Feiwel, publisher

Liz Szabla, editor-in-chief

Rich Deas, creative director

Elizabeth Fithian, marketing director

Barbara Grzeslo, associate art director

Holly West, assistant to the publisher

Dave Barrett, managing editor

Nicole Liebowitz Moulaison, production manager

Jessica Tedder, associate editor

Caroline Sun, publicist

Allison Remcheck, editorial assistant

Ksenia Winnicki, marketing assistant

AVA TREE was edited by Jean Feiwel with Maria Barbo

THE
END

Find out more about our authors and artists and our future publishing at
www.feiwelandfriends.com.

OUR BOOKS ARE FRIENDS FOR LIFE